Abduction
Gone in the Wind

An Icelandic Tale

Nina Olsson

Grosvenor House
Publishing Limited

This book is published by
Grosvenor House Publishing Ltd
Link House
140 The Broadway, Tolworth, Surrey, KT6 7HT.
www.grosvenorhousepublishing.co.uk

This book is a work of fiction. Any resemblance to
people or events, past or present, is purely coincidental.

A CIP record for this book
is available from the British Library

ISBN 978-1-80381-539-8

Rider

This story is a work of fiction.

Apart from the real locations in Iceland, all other references to locations and to persons living or dead are purely coincidental.

Dedication

To all those who are lost and alone, may you find comfort, peace, love and happiness.

Contents

PART ONE – Anna's Story   1

Chapter One – The Barn   3

Chapter Two – The Holiday   5

Chapter Three – Some Weeks Later   8

Chapter Four – Whale Watching   11

Chapter Five – The Blue Lagoon   15

Chapter Six – Making Plans   18

Chapter Seven – The Geysers   21

Chapter Eight – Healing Waters   25

Chapter Nine – The Golden Circle   28

Chapter Ten – Some Concessions   32

Chapter Eleven – Gone in the Wind   35

Chapter Twelve – Journey   37

Chapter Thirteen – New Strategies   41

Chapter Fourteen – Escape   45

Chapter Fifteen – Out!   49

Chapter Sixteen – Saved   52

Chapter Seventeen – Endless Questions   56

Chapter Eighteen – Arrest   60

PART TWO – Christina's Story 65

Chapter Nineteen – First Alerts 67

Chapter Twenty – The Police 72

Chapter Twenty-one – Support from Home 76

Chapter Twenty-two – Home again 80

Chapter Twenty-three – Paul's Return 84

Chapter Twenty-four – News at Last 88

Chapter Twenty-five – Court Case 93

Chapter Twenty-six – Transfer to UK 98

Chapter Twenty-seven – Revelations 102

Acknowledgements 105

Research 106

Author information 107

PART ONE

ANNA'S STORY

CHAPTER ONE

The Barn

The scream when it came was piercingly silent, echoing around the room, the lack of sound bouncing off the walls. I thought my head would burst. He leered across the space between us, his rancid breath filling my nostrils. I told myself not to panic, he enjoyed my fear. I struggled to control my breath, gradually slowing my heart rate.

"Scream," he yelled in my face, "scream, you bitch!"

My mouth was so dry and my throat so tight, I doubted I could scream even if I wanted to. Finally, he lurched out of the room. I sat, glued to the chair, my mind blank. Gradually the numbness wore off and I slowly began to cry.

For a time, I sat in my misery, staring at the walls, where my silent screams had embedded themselves over the past who knew how many weeks. I did not know how long I had been there as the room was kept in darkness, except for the small chink of light that shone through the ill-fitting window frame. It had become my salvation from a journey into madness, as once I had realised its significance, I was able to scratch on the wall when light turned to darkness. When I heard him coming, I would cover it with a rag torn from my clothing.

He would come to the room once in each time period to bring me food. Barely enough to keep me alive, but I knew it was necessary to eat if I were ever to escape this living hell. I dreaded the days he was drunk as I knew he would expect me to perform acts of unspeakable depravity, his stench staying on my body for hours. On his sober days, he would speak to me almost tenderly and I would talk to him, very carefully finding out about my surroundings, allowing the seeds of an escape plan to formulate in my mind.

I asked for another cover, and, in return for certain favours, my request was granted. I needed to keep secret my chink of light from the window frame. I had now begun to chip away at it, so I could see part of the surroundings I was being held in. On the days that my mind was clearer and I was not so paralysed with fear, I thought about what had happened. So small a mistake, a lapse in judgement for which I was paying most dearly.

Chapter Two

The Holiday

The soft whirring noise of the engine accompanied the passenger chatter as the plane flew across the evening sky. "It's so exciting," exclaimed my sister, "I have always wanted to go to Iceland. So do you think that we'll get to see the northern lights?"

"I hope so," I said, "it is the main reason for making the trip, especially at this time of year."

She settled back into her seat, and continued to read her book – appropriately enough, one on Icelandic tales.

I could never read on a moving vehicle of whatever kind, preferring to stare out of the windows, or to sleep – well, catnap – conserving my energies for the arrival at wherever we were going.

Fortunately, the disembarkation, clearing, customs, and eventual arrival at our chosen hotel went more smoothly than I had imagined, and we were finally able to sink into our warm and welcoming beds.

The morning dawned after what seemed like five minutes, and we went for our breakfast. Christina's enthusiasm was undimmed and back in our room we talked about planning an itinerary for the next few days. It hadn't been the best time to visit, the weather being very unsettled, but it was the only time we sisters were both free from our normal life commitments. Besides, we had always wanted to visit Iceland.

We pored over the brochures taken from the hotel lobby. "Well," she said, "what do you fancy doing?"

"Oh, I'm happy to do whatever, as long as it of course includes a night trip out to see the lights."

After an hour of discussion, we had decided on a boat trip to see the whales, a trip to the famous Blue Lagoon, the geyser area, a visit to see where the American and Asian tectonic plates had collided, and, of course, one to hopefully see the aurora borealis. This could not be guaranteed, as the guides, though very good at their jobs I'm sure, did not hold any sway over the weather conditions needed for seeing that particular phenomenon.

We decided to book the trips at the first opportunity, which was on our way out for a walk to get our bearings. "By the time I get all of this clothing on, I'll be too tired to go anywhere," I said breathlessly. Christina laughed and nodded in agreement.

After a quick stop at back at reception to book our trips, we stepped out onto the crisp snow. The sky was blue and clear, and the air cold against our faces, but it was of no trouble to us as we had layer upon layer of clothing on, and good sturdy snow boots. Thus attired, we ventured forth.

We walked for about ten minutes, just long enough to get away from the protective presence of our hotel, when a blizzard sprang up out of nowhere and stopped us in our tracks. We were astonished, there was no warning. We battled on for a short while, but eventually decided that a retreat back to the hotel was the only option.

Once back in our room, we shed our layers and went to the dining room for a hot drink. We had found on other visits to Scandinavian countries that they certainly love their hot chocolate drinks, and we were no different. After half an hour, the skies cleared, so we decided to try our walk again. We again struggled into our cold weather clothing and went out of the door.

The scenario of 'out, short walk, blizzard, back in, hot chocolate' took place four times until we finally gave up any notion of going for a walk. We had been told that 'if you don't like the weather, just wait for five minutes', but we, like the other unsuspecting tourists, thought it was a joke, a slight exaggeration of the climate. We had even seen it written on a T-shirt, but a joke it was not.

We gave up altogether and chose the option of dry clothes, a hot drink, and a chat in the lounge area. "Shall we try again this evening, if the storm stops?" A nod of agreement, and an alternative plan made. We had an afternoon nap.

CHAPTER THREE

Some Weeks Later

I thought back to how it had been when I was first taken there.

The room was cold and I shivered violently. How much of it was from fear, I didn't know. I tried to sleep but to no avail as I was always listening for his step on the stairs. He never spoke to me, just grunts, although I was sure he knew some English but I, of course, knew no Icelandic.

In my less fearful moments I would study my surroundings. The building, though ramshackle, seemed sturdy enough, but here and there I could see cracks where the light shone through the wooden slats. I shuffled over to see if I could see anything of the outside area.

My first attempts were unfruitful as the building backed onto another structure, but finally I was able to see a little of the yard and the fields beyond. A light layer of snow lay over everything, but I could see no footprints. I could hear the sounds of animals but couldn't see them at all. My attention was taken by a pathway just in view at the edge of the building that I now took to be a barn or some type of outhouse. From the changing of the light into darkness, I kept a rough record of how long I had been there.

The stairs creaked, so I hurriedly went back to my place on the floor, slipping my hands into the bindings, which I hoped he wouldn't notice I had loosened. He was in his normal drunken state, growling at me in his uncouth way. I stayed rooted to the spot, not daring to make eye contact as it only served to madden him more. He had brought food and came towards me to loosen the bonds so I could eat. As he grabbed them I struggled too so that it seemed we had both loosed the bindings. He was so drunk he didn't seem to notice.

I couldn't understand why he had abducted me, I was very obviously not a person of wealth, so a ransom demand would not yield very much. I was a tourist, visiting out of season with my sister. I tried not to think of what the other alternatives could be... I was neither young nor beautiful so it had to be he enjoyed exerting power over a helpless person. The thought of it all made me shudder, so I made the noises and signs that I was cold. The food was disgusting-looking, not at all fresh, but then nothing here was fresh-smelling, even the air was fetid. I ate what I could of the food – being weak from hunger wouldn't help me in any escape plans. He staggered about and was clearly looking for something. I kept my head down, but stared at what I could from under hooded eyes.

After a while he grunted at me, and in his clumsy way retied my bindings. I held my wrists as taut as I could, knowing that the straps would loosen off when I relaxed. He staggered out of the loft, and left me to my thoughts and fears. I had tried to give myself some sort of normality after the blind panic of the first couple of days. Surely someone would be looking for me by now, although where they would start was anyone's guess. I tried hard to think if I had seen any cameras at the coach rest stop. But the weather had been so bad it was unlikely that, even if they had been present, they would have shown anything useful. He had taken my mobile phone and thrown it into a snowdrift on the side of the road, so there would be no location marker. I felt thoroughly bereft, except for the fact that I knew my sister would not rest until she had some answers. She was a veritable 'dog with a bone' once she got her teeth into something.

I decided to try to sleep, if I could. Usually it would be some time before he came to check on me. I worked my hands free again, and even though I was cramped and cold, I could get into a more comfortable position.

CHAPTER FOUR

Whale Watching

"Glad we started off early, it's a long way along this coastal road, and the deep snow makes it really heavy going."

"Oh, it's not so bad," said my ultra-fit sister, who even at this early hour was bursting with energy.

We were on our way to the boat dock, our trip today being out to the bay to see some whales, if we were lucky. We were thoroughly enjoying our short holiday here in Iceland; the only slightly negative was the constantly changing weather. To be fair, we had been warned, and, as said, had even seen some T-shirts with typical Icelandic humour, which read 'if you don't like the weather, just wait five minutes'. That about summed it up.

However, we were warm in our appropriate clothing, even though it made walking a little more difficult and slow. We finally turned into the small boatyard and walked along to the ship berthed at the end of the quay. It was smaller than I had imagined and I idly wondered how well it would cope with the choppy seas out in the bay. Still, if the whales could cope, so could we.

"Tickets, please!" shouted the young lady at the foot of the gangplank. So we tourists, who had huddled together like a group of penguins, moved slowly forward, towards the open mouth of the ship, before disappearing into the bowels of the iron monster.

"It's going to be very rough, I think," said Christina. "Just as well I have taken my seasickness pills."

So, not so ultra-fit after all, I thought with a tinge of satisfaction. I never suffered from anything like that.

We were all taken to a large room where we were given warm drinks and a talk on what we might see. It all sounded fascinating. Of course, there was a small proviso built in – that we may not see any whales at all – but that risk was understood when booking the trip.

Once underway, we found seats on the deck and sat, taking some photographs, slowly taking on the appearance of icebergs as the wind blew in a thin layer of snow that covered everyone, very quickly turning to ice. We laughed quietly as we surveyed others, some slowly taking on the shape of polar bears, at least those who did not move around.

Further out into the bay, people flooded out onto the decks.

Boy was it cold, actually that was an understatement, it was absolutely freezing. However, the promise of what we might see made it feel worthwhile. After we had been sailing for a while, we came to a likely area and the boat virtually stopped.

A few hardy souls, including us, stood and patiently scanned the dark waters for any sign of marine life. The taking of photographs was now our main priority. We watched intently and were treated to a few dark fins in the water. However, they were not from whales, but from playful dolphins. This, to me anyway, was just as much of a treat, and I clicked happily away on my camera, until my hands – and everything else for that matter – were too cold to function. We went back inside where another hot drink awaited, which we gratefully imbibed.

The journey back to Reykjavik harbour was uneventful, though the wind still made the sea very choppy, and even more snow fell. Our walk back to our hotel was of an even slower pace, but we did stop to photograph the Viking longship sculpture on the shore road. The snow, in its very helpful way, got heavier and heavier. I remarked to my sister that I was glad we were just visitors, as I wouldn't want to live there permanently. Although perhaps if you did, you would get used to the constantly changing weather conditions.

Back at the hotel, after a warm drink and some hot food, we started to plan our next trip. As we were only there a few days, we wanted to fill our time, weather conditions notwithstanding. We decided on a coach trip out to the Blue Lagoon. An absolutely 'must have' experience. A special place made from hot springs, where you could bathe in the warm waters. I wasn't quite sure how I felt about that – being in a swimming costume in an outdoor area surrounded by lava rocks covered in snow. It seemed such a contradiction in terms.

I checked through my photographs before bed, glad that I had been able to get some dolphin pictures, but sorry to have missed out on the whales. Still, our Icelandic visit was proving to be most interesting and we still had a number of trips left, including the ones to the geysers, and the Golden Circle trip to see where the American and European tectonic plates crashed up against each other. That sounded more appealing to me than wading about half-naked in a thermal pool, but I had promised my sister I would go. I just hoped that the lagoon lived up to its name and reputation.

Chapter Five

The Blue Lagoon

The journey out to the lagoon area wasn't too far, it being situated on the Reykjanes Peninsula. This, we were told, was a geothermal spa near Grindavik, situated in a lava field, in front of Mount Þorbjörn.

A different crowd of people were on the coach, quite a number of young couples. Christina and I took our seats, and we were off. The countryside mostly consisted of snow-covered lava fields, which I found most interesting. I liked to think about how they had been formed, how old they might be, and also I enjoyed taking photographs of the stark images, many of my pictures being black and white anyway. I could hear the guide's voice in the background telling us all the various bits of information, including the rules of the venue.

We arrived at the complex and were told that the coach would be leaving in four hours, and where to meet up. We were assured this was plenty of time for the spa experience. We were shown to the changing rooms, where we stripped and had to shower naked, removing any foreign particles that we may have brought in with us. Once in our bathing suits, it was outside and along a wooden jetty, then down into the waters. It was so cold getting from the changing rooms into the water, but once there, you were enveloped in what felt like a warm blanket. Just deep enough to cover my shoulders, my toes squelching in the soft white mud at the bottom, I luxuriated in the warm and, in some places, hot water. It was bliss. A bar had been set up on a floating platform and people mostly stood about in little groups, chatting.

Any worries I had about going in the waters soon dissipated, as I gradually warmed up to my core. There was a light snowfall and it felt completely incongruous to be sitting in what amounted to be a very warm bath, in a snow-covered lava field, with light snow covering my head. A very strange feeling.

The thought of having to get out and back to the changing rooms was daunting, but in actual fact was no problem, as being warmed to your core meant your body stayed warm for a while – at least long enough for a shower and to get dressed again. A bizarre experience all around, but I loved it, as did Christina.

In the cafe area, drinking certainly my now favourite drink – hot chocolate – we sisters talked about our time in Iceland, and how much we were enjoying it, despite what the weather was throwing at us. We were, of course, prepared for that – it was early February after all, and the name of the country had given us a clue.

We still had another trip to look forward to, then a day sightseeing around Reykjavik and later a flight home. In the evening, in the hotel bar area, we met up with a couple who had also been on the coach, so we spent a happy couple of hours with them, all of us recounting our Icelandic adventures so far.

When Christina and I first talked about a short holiday in Iceland, I wasn't sure. I like cold weather, yes, but that much cold? Still, we did have appropriate clothing. My doubts came to nothing, as I had thoroughly enjoyed everything we had done so far, and didn't think our last couple of days would be any different. I couldn't have been more wrong.

We both slept well, awoke ready for a good breakfast, and went to see if our trip was still on, as the weather hadn't sounded too promising.

Chapter Six

Making Plans

He and I seemed to have settled into a sort of bizarre routine. He would bring me food at random times, but I figured it was at least once a day. Working from that premise, I could begin to work out some sort of measurement of the days.

I scratched a code out on the wooden slat, 'N' for night and 'D' for day. I guessed at how long I had been there for the first weeks, before my head had started to rule my emotions and my panic had subsided. I was still alive, and had learnt to endure all the indignities he subjected me to each day.

I slowly built up my calendar, and my rudimentary clock for time-keeping.

From the crack in the timbers, I could see that the landscape was changing, albeit very slowly. The snow on the ground looked less deep and the few horses I could see were moving more freely. I decided that it must be March or very early April, and if that were the case, I had been there at least two months. Even if that assumption was incorrect, it at least gave me a start point.

He had given me a few concessions, an extra blanket, food that was more palatable, but I longed for a bath and a change of clothes, as I now smelt as bad as he did. However, I knew I would have to work very slowly and carefully on that.

His demands on my body had lessened, fortunately he was drunk most of the time and in latter days had only stayed in the room long enough to shove the food at me.

I did, however, realise that this was a far more dangerous time for me, as he may decide at any moment that I was not worth keeping, and go off in search of another victim.

It helped a great deal that I could free my hands, and that I could move around a little. I still, of course, went through the pretence of being tied up. He would remove the ropes to allow me to eat and drink.

I was waiting for a time when he would forget to redo my bonds, although I had already found a way of slipping them off. Very occasionally, I would try to talk to him, feigning great interest in Icelandic culture. He has started to talk to me more, so I asked him to teach me some Icelandic words. Even drunk, his English was pretty good. I was very deliberate in what I chose to be taught, only so much each time, all seemingly random, but in fact, I was piecing together a picture of my location and surroundings.

I still submitted to his demands, pretending to fight with him, which I had realised was what he wanted.

He needed to exert absolute power over me, but in my head, he was submitting to my quest for information, which gave me power over him, and a small degree of comfort.

A few more weeks passed, and with it the strong desire to get free of him and this awful place. I would use the extra blanket and any other materials as clothing. The snow was still on the ground, and I didn't know for how much longer, and after everything I didn't want to die of hypothermia. I still did not know how far I was from any other habitation, as I could see only the small yard from my 'window', and the corner of a field.

I decided to be brave and ask if we could go outside as I longed to see the sky. I knew it would come at a price, but I decided it would be worth it if I gained my wish. The first time of asking was a definite no, but later he relented and agreed. He would need to untie me, and to give me back my shoes. He threatened me with punishment if I should try any stupid moves, like trying to escape. I assured him that I wouldn't, besides which, it wasn't part of my plan just yet. This was all an exercise to see how far I could go in my requests, to see where I was, and the lay of the countryside.

Chapter Seven

The Geysers

I woke early and crept to the window, not wanting to wake Christina. The hotel overlooked the main promenade and at first there was little going on save for the occasional car heading to the cargo terminal.

Some movement caught my eye, and to my amazement six joggers came past, moving through the snow as if it wasn't there. I looked at my watch – 6:30am and still quite dark – were they mad! No wonder they are all such hardy people, well that and all the fish that is on every menu. I went back to bed. Just watching them was enough exercise for me.

I must have slept for another couple of hours and awoke to see Christina up and about. I told her about the joggers, and we both decided that, yes, they were mad.

Over breakfast we discussed the day's itinerary. We were going on a coach trip, out to see the geyser region. These were the stuff of myths and legends, and Iceland certainly had plenty of those. I had learnt about such things at school, and was about to see them in reality. I was very much looking forward to today's trip.

Back in our room we donned our waterproof clothing, especially our over-trousers and boots, then, with cameras at the ready, we found our coach party in the hotel foyer. There are certain, not-to-be-missed things to do in Iceland, and this was one of them.

We carried our coats as we would be too hot on the coach. There was a lot of excited chatter as the coach pulled away from the hotel. Due to the fickleness of the weather, we were not always sure if the planned trip would take place. Some of the other coach companies had already cancelled various trips, but we had been lucky so far.

It was an early start, as the hours of daylight were limited. We chatted as the coach made its way through Reykjavik and the outlying areas. I found the different types of housing areas fascinating, the houses becoming much more traditional as we left the city boundaries.

The road went out into the countryside, heading towards Haukadalur and the Laugarfjall hill. We passed near the village of Thingvellir, stopping for a photo opportunity. We took some, but we knew we were going there the next day on the Golden Circle trip, and would have plenty of time then.

I slept then for a while, as I often do on moving vehicles, and woke up as we were pulling into a parking area. From then on, it was on foot. There were a number of coaches there too, spilling their bundles of camera-carrying tourists.

The main attractions were Great Geysir and Old Strokkur (The Churn), but there were also a number of smaller geysers and mud pools dotted around the rough but imposing landscape. Large groups were already gathered mostly around Strokkur, as it burst into life every few minutes, whereas the wait for Geysir was much longer, if at all. It was not long before Strokkur started to put on a show and do what it was famous for.

Its centre began to bubble, the icy blue water becoming more and more agitated, until a huge plume of gas and water rose up into the air. It must have been 80 feet at least. We all gasped, it was magnificent. We all stood in awe while Strokkur performed, time after time. We watched the spectacle again and again, before wandering around the site, and eventually returning to the coach.

The conversation on the way back spoke of the majesty of the sights we had seen. However, this was not to be the end of this amazing day. On the way back, the guide explained how the phenomenon took place. Apparently, the area was a wide strip of land, aligned in the direction of the tectonic plates, which we were to see the following day. It was, he told us, an active geothermal area, which we were aware of, having been to the Blue Lagoon. He was a bit more technical and told us that the eruptions were caused by the ground water coming into contact with the hot bedrock. This would then heat up, building up temperature and pressure, which, when it reached its peak, erupted.

The geysers were thought to have been in existence for around 10,000 years. I tried to imagine that, whose eyes would have seen them over the centuries. The first written evidence of the Great Geysir was from 1294 – just imagine that. I loved learning about places I visited.

We were still excitedly talking about what we had seen, and in some instances photographed, over our meal at the hotel. We had what we hoped would be an interesting evening planned, as we were being taken out to a dark, isolated area where there would be no light pollution, to see the northern lights, also known as the aurora borealis.

Sadly they turned out to be as elusive as the whales. They wouldn't be seen after all – cloud cover obliterated everything. But never mind, it was never guaranteed, and was just a tantalising gesture of great riches to come, at the moment lying hidden.

We weren't too disappointed as we had already tried in other Scandinavian countries, but we were hopeful that somewhere, at some other time, we would see them in their full glory. Besides which, we had had a pretty amazing day at the geyser area.

Chapter Eight

Healing Waters

Things seemed to be improving and I tried my best to be convincingly submissive.

My next request was for a bath, which of course meant going into the house. How to approach this? I had to be very patient and careful.

I knew that any request would come with a 'price tag', but I suppose my body and I were becoming used to that, and I had found a way of detaching my mind, so that it was not actually me who was being violated. It seemed to be working well thus far, helped by the fact that he always had some alcohol before he came to the loft, and the attack was mercifully short-lived.

My request was met with some surprise, but after a few days, it was granted. I was untied and again my life threatened if I should even think of escape. However, this was not my immediate plan as I needed more information. It would be pointless getting away, then dying in the snow.

The main house was a surprise to me. Though dirty and neglected, it must at some time have had a woman's touch; it was certainly not the home of a bachelor. I wanted to ask, but decided that now was not the time. The bathroom was cold, but the water was warm, and though I had to suffer the indignity of him watching, I relaxed into the cleansing water. My heart soared, it was the first time I had felt human for weeks.

At one point, he disappeared off and returned with towels and a bathrobe. I mouthed my thanks and reluctantly stepped out of the comforting waters.

My hair and body now clean, I felt so much better. He had also brought some clothes, not exactly my size but serviceable. They must have belonged to a wife or perhaps mother, I wasn't sure which, and certainly wasn't going to ask. Once back in the main room, he tied me to a chair and disappeared off for some time. I was pleased as it gave me the opportunity to have a good look around the room, and some views of the outside from the small windows.

On his return, I could also see he had been in the bath, washed his hair and tidied his beard. He didn't look like the same person. I had to stop myself being complimentary to him. Our relationship, such as it was, was built on my fear and him being in total control, so I needed to remember that. I did not want to shift the balance until I was absolutely ready to make my escape.

He untied me and instead of taking me back to the loft, took me to his bed. The inevitable happened, yet it had almost a feel of tenderness to it and I responded best I could. I was still his hostage. I did, however, tell him my name, and asked his.

At first he didn't reply and I feared I had overstepped the mark and the old fear began to creep in again. Eventually he said it was Einar. Whether or not that was his real name, I didn't know, but at least it was a start.

It was time to go back to the loft and he seemed almost sorry. I assured him that I would not run as I had nowhere to go, and didn't know where I was anyway. He seemed satisfied with that and left me untied. Then, with his threats ringing in my ears, he left.

I knew now that there was at least some level on which I could reach him, and continued to slowly make my plans. I also knew that I would have to be extremely careful as he was very unpredictable.

Several visits followed, but the levels of aggression had certainly changed and in some bizarre way I started to feel sorry for him. I wished I knew more of his backstory, so, to this end, I would have to gather any further information with extreme caution.

CHAPTER NINE

The Golden Circle

An early start, not yet light. Breakfast done, then to the reception desk to check if the trip was still running. There were some disappointed tourists, but not us. Our trip was on.

We were to be traversing the Golden Circle, to see where the American and Eurasian tectonic plates met. The wind and slight snowfall had not put our driver off. Daylight hours were at a premium, hence the early start. Full sunrise was to be around 10am, but we hoped to be an hour underway by then. According to the weather reports, our guide informed us, there was to be some wind and sleet-type rainfall, but nothing that we would not be able to cope with, especially having been subjected to the various weather conditions already thrown at us since we arrived. The country was called Iceland after all, and for good reason.

We were expecting about seven hours of daylight. The coach was full; Christina and I took our seats. We started off and as we reached the outskirts of the city, light was peeping over the horizon. The snow flurry stopped and we settled back to watch the countryside flying by us, the cityscape giving way to outlying houses, then to miles of snow-covered rocky terrain. Much as I liked to look at the view, it was certainly not on my list of places to live.

The journey took what seemed like hours. In our rush to get ready early, I had forgotten my watch, and Christina never wore one. I suppose we could have looked on our phones, but decided that we wanted a day free of self-imposed time constraints. We finally reached our destination, a large car and coach parking area where we and the other brave or, perhaps, foolhardy folk gathered.

From here onwards, the journey was on foot to the gorge where we were able to walk through the space between the two rocky outcrop areas. It was bitterly cold, but the effort of walking in our heavy but warm clothing soon heated us up. A very small snowplough was driving through the walkway clearing away any loose snow. It was not a road as such, and certainly not wide enough for any conventional vehicle.

The scenery was spectacular in its own way, the lava-scarred Reykjanes Peninsula was made all the more amazing when you thought of what was really going on here. This place was the coming together of the western side of the Eurasian and the eastern side of the North American tectonic plates. This colossal happening had brought chaos in its wake, resulting in many volcanic eruptions and earthquakes. It took quite some time to walk through the gap, and at the other end was a small cafe where I stayed drinking my favourite drink while Christina went off to take photographs.

Even though it was quite barren, the landscape had its own kind of beauty. It was such an amazing feeling knowing that you had been walking between two great continents, in the only place on earth where the plates made landfall. It made me feel very insignificant, but lucky to be seeing such majesty.

The wonderment of the area seeped into your very being, but unfortunately so did the cold and I, for one, having left the warmth of the cafe, felt the need for the warmth of the coach. Once everyone was back on board, we were taken for a scenic trip around the area, the guide filling us in with the geological information.

The time was moving on, and the sky began to darken quite dramatically. The wind had picked up and was blowing strongly and increasing steadily. We were not worried as we all had great faith in our Icelandic driver, a large, quiet man, but with an air of being able to cope with anything. The thought of any danger was not in our minds.

After a little time, whilst still up in the hills, we could see a blue light winking in the distance. The snowfall had turned an icy rain, and the wind speed had increased quite significantly, buffeting the coach. When we finally reached the crossroads, a police car was blocking the road and the driver was told that all roads had been closed and to await further instructions from the police before proceeding.

We were directed to a large parking area where there were a number of other coaches. There was a cafe, a petrol station, and a small number of shops on the complex, and a hotel on the other side of the road.

Christina and the other passengers got off the coach, she feeling the need for a cup of coffee. However, I decided to stay on board. In my naivety, I thought we wouldn't be there too long, also I was warm and sleepy and had felt, unusually, a little travel sick, so did go to sleep once the coach had emptied. I also didn't take into account the worsening weather.

I awoke some time later, needing as always the toilet, and so endeavoured to get off the coach. The rain was very heavy and the wind unbelievably strong as I stepped down on to the gravel. The doors of the coach closed behind me, stopping me getting back on, so I had no choice but to fight my way to the cafe at the other end of the car park.

There wasn't a soul about, but I could hear the sounds of many voices coming from the brightly lit cafe, so very unsteadily I started towards the welcoming place of shelter.

CHAPTER TEN

Some Concessions

Some time after the cold and darkness of the winter months, the weather started to slowly change, and with it, his mood.

I had been allowed up to the farmhouse on a couple of occasions, which I savoured as I was able to clean my body, and, to a certain degree, clear my mind. He also started to drink less and to tidy himself up. However, I felt more than ever at risk. He may miss the ego trip, and the absolute power over me, and decide at any time to look for it elsewhere, and think that I was no longer needed.

His demands on me were less aggressive, but he was still a threat, and I made sure that I complied to his wishes. His presence was still frightening, and my disgust still the same. I put up just a little resistance, keeping the balance of power on his side. A fine line hovered between my salvation and oblivion.

I would often think back to the moment where I, against all of my instincts, made my fateful decision. I wondered if the police were searching for me. What would my family be going through, not knowing if I was alive or dead? I shuddered at the thoughts.

I did not hold out any hope of there being any CCTV footage from the area as the storm would have obscured any usable images. Also the cameras were mostly restricted to the town areas. Following the 2015 murder case, more had been installed, but it was unlikely there would be many at the coach stop, and also, he would, I'm sure, know where they were, and would avoid them. No, my only hope was in myself and escape.

Something must have happened because one night he arrived at the loft, very drunk, and assaulted me in a most violent fashion. No words were spoken, and after the thankfully short but injurious onslaught, he left.

I was stunned and spent much of the time afterwards trying to work out if I had betrayed my intentions in any way. Finally, bruised and very upset, I cried myself to sleep.

The next day, he appeared, quiet and, I think, a little remorseful. He invited me into the house. When I felt it was the right time, I asked him if I had upset him, and if so, I was very sorry. I still needed to play the submissive role, and it was important that he believed in my compliance.

He said very little, so I decided it was best to be quiet. We sat in his kitchen, looking at each other. I didn't really know why I was there, and he was in a silent mood. After a while, I stared out of the window.

I could see that the snow was starting to melt, and I guessed that I must have been there about three months. I could feel my mood getting lower, so I told myself silently that I must not give up. Surely things would improve in the spring.

I didn't know if this was his farm, or just a place where he was, perhaps, a caretaker. The only livestock I had seen were some horses that I had glimpsed from the loft when I first arrived. I plucked up my courage and spoke to him as pleasantly as I could.

I asked had he lived in this place for long, and to my surprise, he answered. It had been his parents' farm, both of whom were now dead. He and his brother had taken over the management of the place, until his brother left to work in Reykjavik, and later left the country. Farming had never been his choice, but he had been left with it, and he was very resentful – that, I could see. I wanted to ask more about the brother, but knew not to, as I felt strongly that it would provoke an angry outburst. Besides there seemed to be something else connected with it all.

A further period of silence ensued, during which I looked around the room. There were some personal items on show, though not many, and certainly no family photographs. Not at all much to build up a picture of the man or his life. After a while, he asked if I would like a bath, and even knowing what would be expected afterwards, I gratefully said yes. At least for the short time in the warm waters, I was left alone with my thoughts and my plans.

I desperately needed to work out how all of this had happened and why I was in this nightmare situation.

Chapter Eleven

Gone in the Wind

I stopped, deciding what would be the best way to reach the cafe, but my progress was pitifully slow and I had resorted to clinging on to one of the lampposts lighting up the car park. I had left my handbag, camera and other things on my seat, bringing only my coat and my purse in the pocket. I realised that I would need both hands to help me in case I fell.

It was fairly well lit, and as I looked around I was aware of no one else about, the car park was deserted. If the coach drivers were in their coaches, they were probably eating, or having a rest.

Come on, I said to myself, *this isn't going to get you up to the cafe*. I didn't expect Christina to come looking for me as she thought I was asleep on the coach. Also, who besides me would be foolhardy enough to be wandering about in this storm.

I tried letting go of the lamppost and was nearly blown over. There were several flagpoles around the area, the flags of which were flying absolutely horizontally. I started to feel panic taking hold of me.

Somewhere in the car park, some headlights came on and in the gloom a large shape came towards me. One of those 4x4 monsters. As it drew level with me, the window went down, and the occupant spoke to me, in English. *Strange*, I thought, *how would they know?* But then, of course, this was a tourist area, so chances of English being understood would be high.

His words were drowned out by the high wind, so he gestured for me to get into the car. At first, I said no.

Thinking that I didn't understand, he shouted, "It's OK, I'll take you to the cafe."

My need for warmth and to get out of the howling wind and torrential rain overrode my normal cautiousness and good sense, so gratefully I got into the car.

He smiled at me, a man in his 50s, I guess, but looking pleasant enough. He drove around the car park towards the cafe entrance. As we drew near to the door, he slowed down, then suddenly I heard the car doors lock as the car slowly moved off from the cafe. I asked what was happening, as the car gathered speed and we left the car park.

In the distance, I could still see the blue flashing lights of the police car, but we turned off and went in the opposite direction. I shouted to be let out, and he pulled over on the empty highway, but instead of releasing me, his whole demeanour changed and he punched me.

I must have blacked out as I don't remember anything else, until I awoke some time later.

Chapter Twelve

Journey

I woke up with a headache, the like of which I couldn't remember. "Chris, how long have I been asleep?" There was no answer. In my half-waking state, I could feel the movement of the coach as we drove along the dark roads.

I asked again, this time more awake, and to my horror, realised that I was in a car. My hands were bound and there was a faint hospital-like smell in the air. I looked across at the driver, and, at first, recollection eluded me. Many questions flooded my mind. *Where was I? How did I get here? Who was this man?* I turned to speak with him, but was met with a growl that left no uncertainty that my questions were not welcome.

I was covered by a blanket, hiding the fact that I was bound – not only my hands – but to the chair itself. I was shocked and my mind went into overdrive trying to make sense of the situation.

Eventually he spoke and told me to act normally if we saw any other cars or he would lock me in the boot. I was too frightened to do anything but comply.

When I had awoken, I had believed that I was on the coach and we were on our way back to Reykjavik, the roads having been reopened. I sat very quietly in the front seat of the car, trying to make some sense of my surroundings.

At first, it was very dark. We passed the occasional snowplough working to keep the roads open. I tried to think of a way to alert them, but to no avail, as my movements were severely restricted. Besides which, snuggled in the blanket, we must have looked like a couple returning home for the night.

We drove for a very long time and I must have gone back to sleep. With help, I don't know, but sleep I did. The second time I awoke, the first tinges of dawn were lighting the sky. I had no ideas of the time, as daylight hours were very short this time of year, and it wasn't actually quite light yet. Dark shapes appeared out of the gloom – perhaps buildings, farms maybe – as we drove past, but the rest of the landscape appeared empty apart from the glow of the snow in the headlights.

What had happened? I could not calm my thoughts down enough to try to make some sense of anything. I tried very hard not to let my fear take over all rational thought, but rather concentrate on the little I did know, and could make out from the car windows. What I did see did not fill me with any hope.

The smell, I decided, was like chloroform. I had worked in hospitals as an auxiliary nurse. Of course, chloroform was no longer in use, but its distinctive smell, I remembered. No wonder I had such a headache and was so disorientated.

We drove on. I reckoned that it must have been at least four to five hours, if not more. We went past what I took to be a lake, its dark surface shimmering with what little light there was. There was no activity anywhere. Calmer now, I began to make a mental note of what I could see of the surroundings, to be used in the faint hope of escaping this nightmare.

We rumbled along at a decent pace so as not to alert any of the early morning passing workers. The road became narrower, like our English B roads, until it turned off into a track. Silent figures watched us from the fields, and I could just about make out that they were animals, either horses or cows. Horses I think.

Eventually we came to a ramshackle-looking house with a barn-type building standing next to it. We were miles from anywhere, and there wasn't a living soul around. We stopped, and he grunted at me to get out of the car once untied. My limbs were cramped and ached from being in the same position for so long. I was in too much pain to even think of escape, besides which, I could not clear my head enough to devise any plans. I think that I had become resigned to my fate, and did not want my last hours to be fraught.

I was taken to the barn building, where there was a makeshift room in the loft, up a very unsafe-looking ladder, with a crude cot inside. He pushed me into the room, my hands still bound. I indicated to him that

I needed to pass urine, and had to suffer the indignity of him watching whilst I used a bucket in the corner of the room. For this he untied me, then afterwards retied my hands, before flinging me down on to what I thought was a cot, but was in fact a dirty mattress on the floor.

Before I could speak, he left the room, whereupon the full weight of the situation hit me and I wept waves of tears, fuelled by my fear and hopelessness.

He returned some time later with a small amount of food and a blanket. He was reeking of alcohol. He removed my shoes and took my coat. My true nightmare was about to begin.

Chapter Thirteen

New Strategies

I started to feel much stronger and had become more used to the awful food I was being given. I knew that I had to eat and drink to increase my strength, to allow me to escape. I also knew that I had to continue playing the subservient female and not appear to be too insistent in any of my requests.

My infrequent visits up to the house allowed me to get some bearings, although all I could see at present were fields and pockets of lava outcrops, dark against the landscape. At night, in the loft, I would try to make sense of the star patterns I could see through the cracks I had made in the old wooden slats.

I figured that we had driven quite a way north, and whilst feigning unconsciousness, I had seen a lake. I tried really hard to get some bearings so that when I did manage to get free, I would not get further lost in the very inhospitable landscape. This was very difficult as the effects of the chloroform had, at first, clouded my mind.

I was now sure there had been a female at the house at some point, as there appeared to be odd touches of a woman's hand, certainly in the very odd choices of pictures and paintings in the house. They didn't look to me as the sort of things that a hardened bachelor would choose. However, I was very careful not to make mention of anything too personal, his moods were still very unpredictable and I was still subject to the occasional outburst.

The sky had lightened and I was able to see more from my loft. Spring was on the way and the snow was only evident on the tops of the rock outcrops.

Submitting to yet another ordeal, I was able to talk my way back into the house the next day. This time I paid particular notice to the paintings. They were, I reasoned, of local places, the terrain looking very much like that I could see from my loft.

He left the room, and I was able to study one of them, close up. The artist had signed it, but also named it Ásbyrgi, which I reckoned to be a place fairly nearby. I vaguely remembered some talk of it at the hotel when some tourists, on some sort of driving/walking trip around the country, spoke of it. How I wished I had listened more, or at least remembered where it was.

He had come back into the room. I had sat down near the fireplace. He said gruffly, "Water ready for bath, but first please me." It was becoming increasingly hard to mask my repulsion of him, but I knew pretence would be my only salvation.

Later, his lust sated, and myself cleansed in the warm waters, we sat, almost like an old married couple in the dingy room. It was getting harder and harder to go back to the draughty loft, but I knew I couldn't stay in the house where he was more aware of my movements.

I idly wondered if anyone was still searching for me or had now given up. It now had to be more than four months by my reckoning, although I wasn't sure of an exact timescale. It appeared to be spring, no longer snowing, and the days were getting lighter and longer.

Thankfully, he had stopped watching me dress after my bath, so I took the opportunity to rifle through the wardrobe and take an extra pair of pants, which I put on under my clothes. I would need the extra warmth as it was still reasonably cold, my fitness levels were low, and I had lost weight. At any other time, the weight thing would have pleased me, but this was not the time. I needed all my strength.

Back in my loft, I hoped he would leave me alone, at least for a few hours, so I could rest and formulate my plans. He would be back later with the meagre sustenance, then hopefully leave me be for the rest of the night. He had started to leave my hands unbound, but of course the door to the loft was firmly locked, as was the main door to the barn. The ladder down to the floor below was very rickety, so had to be negotiated very carefully. One slip could easily result in a broken leg, or worse.

I thought about my home more and more, and my husband, Michael, and son, Paul, also about my sister and her family, Adam and Martin. How must she be coping? At least she had her family around her. How I longed for that. I began to cry, softly at first, then with great racking sobs that I found hard to control. It had been a long time since I had cried, having become numb to the situation I was in. My mind went over and over what had happened, and how it could have happened. How could I have been so stupid? Too trusting, I suppose, as obviously it hadn't occurred to me that the kind man offering me the lift would have meant me any harm.

On reflection, I think it was a spur of the moment act, as things at the farm were not laid out as a hiding place for a kidnap victim, but there was the issue of the mattress on the floor. Perhaps the motive was purely rape and murder, with no need for a hiding place. I tortured myself with such thoughts until I finally fell asleep.

Come morning, I resolved to make my escape. Whatever his motives, his behaviour was becoming more erratic and I knew I had to get away.

CHAPTER FOURTEEN

Escape

I heard movement down in the barn and decided that if I was going to act, it needed to be now.

His behaviour had worried me greatly of late, he was so unpredictable, and I had again begun to fear for my life. He had stopped binding my hands and had allowed me to keep my shoes with me. I had done my very best to play the subservient role, gaining what little trust I could. I resolved that it must be now that I put my plans into operation.

I could hear him breathing heavily as he came up the ladder, and I hoped that in some ways, he had been drinking as it would make him unsteady on his feet. I stretched myself, and stood in readiness behind the door. I could hear him fumbling for the key, and then the clicking sound as it turned in the lock. The door opened inwards towards me, and as it opened, I moved into the space. He wasn't expecting me to be there as surprise flickered across his face. In that moment, I reached across the gap, and pushed him with all of my might.

Because of the unexpectedness of the attack, he was caught off guard and off balance. He instinctively lifted a hand to defend himself and in so doing, lost his grip on the ladder, and fell. I hurried down the ladder whilst he was not moving and found a hammer on his workbench, which I used to give him a blow to his head. I didn't have a great deal of strength, so I knew he wouldn't be knocked out for long.

My mind went into overdrive and all I could think of was self-preservation. I looked around for something else, my plan being to disable the car. I picked up a hunting knife and began slashing away at the tyres on the car. I just needed to make sure he couldn't follow me. There was a lot of blood and I thought it seemed a lot for a head wound. At first he groaned a lot, then there was silence. I had originally thought of taking the car, but didn't know where the keys were, and didn't want to spend time looking for them in case he woke up. Then my fate would truly have been sealed. Nothing for it but to slash the tyres. Everything became a blur.

On my way out of the barn, I saw his old work coat hanging on a hook, which I took to keep me warm. Into its deep pockets I put the hammer and the knife – weapons to defend myself when he came after me.

The narrow track ran up from the front of the house, so I started along it, remembering vaguely that a road ran across the top of it. I hoped so… It seemed so long since I had been brought to this living hell. I listened desperately for the sounds of a vehicle, but there was nothing but silence. This was most certainly a forsaken area. I wandered along the track and decided that I needed to get rid of the hammer. My mind was clearer now, and my body full of adrenaline. The hammer was evidence, and I would need to get rid of it. I had seen enough crime dramas on the TV to know how things worked. I saw a small copse on the side of the track. The ground was still quite hard, but I managed to dig a hole with the knife, just deep enough to bury the hammer.

There was still the question of the knife, but I decided that I might need it, and could dispose of it later.

I thought back to the chain of events bringing me to this moment, and I was pleased with myself that I had finally had the will and strength to fight back. He had put me through unspeakable horrors, and even his more tender moments had not compensated for all that had happened. Fear is a strange thing, at first paralysing, then hardening your resolve. I had absolutely no idea that stepping into that vehicle, on that stormy night, would have such a terrifying outcome.

Thinking of everyone at home helped quicken my step. I was still listening intently for any vehicle sounds, but there was nothing as yet. I thought about what had taken place in the barn, and about attacking him and the vehicle. Now I needed to get far away from the house, and when I felt safer, to deal with the knife.

Some time later, I saw a small outcrop of rocks on the opposite side of the road, so I went to look for a suitable burial site for the knife. The blade was already covered in soil from when I got rid of the hammer, but I was surprised to see red colouration near the handle. Were my eyes playing tricks?

In amongst the rocks was an area of undergrowth where I was able to dig to a reasonable depth. I inserted the knife in an upright position, then covered over the area with soil and scrub material.

The deed completed, I crossed back to the original side of the road, and continued walking. I felt a curious lightness in my being, and finally a belief that I would be rescued.

CHAPTER FIFTEEN

Out!

I was out.

I had hurried the best I could down to the roads leading away from the house, towards what I hoped would be freedom. I knew that this was a very dangerous time; he could follow me at any point. I had taken the knife from the workbench, and I knew I had slashed the tyres on the 4x4. No easy task in my weakened state. Still, I couldn't rest as he may have had a second vehicle.

It was so bleak and cold, but hopefully it would warm up throughout the day. I had taken his padded jacket, but the pants I wore were of a very thin material. Fortunately, I was still full of adrenaline, and didn't feel much other than the overriding desire to be free of him, the farmhouse, and the whole nightmare.

When I had finally reached the crossroads, I was undecided as to which way to go. I thought about the painting I had seen and looked desperately for any familiar parts of the landscape. In the far distance I could see what looked to be a tree line, and decided to head towards them. The sides of the road afforded a little cover, so with great trepidation I started along it, straining my ears for the sounds of any vehicles.

Even if one came along, I couldn't be sure it wasn't him, so would have to stay hidden until it had passed. I walked for what seemed like hours, but of course, in my poor state, I didn't cover much distance. The trees seemed as far away as when I had started. I had to stop frequently for short rests.

I should have planned things better, like for instance bringing enough food, and particularly water, but him falling from the ladder had been opportune, and I took full advantage to make my escape. There was no traffic, this was still early in the year, and not exactly a tourist area, but I was hopeful there would be someone around to help. I plodded on. The sun by now was fully up, so I reckoned it was about midday. I thought that it must be around the month of May, looking at the evidence of spring around me, and also I had tried to keep a tally of the number of days that I had been there. It was a bit of a guess, as the first few weeks I was too frightened to think of anything.

In the distance I heard a noise, and immediately dived for cover behind a large rock. The vehicle came nearer and as it passed I could hear children's voices from a partially open window. A sadly missed opportunity, but then I couldn't have been sure as to who was in the vehicle.

Where were they going? Perhaps they were from one of the farms, or perhaps out for a picnic somewhere. I hoped it was the latter. I doggedly carried on. My mind at first had been in absolute turmoil. Would he stay unconscious long enough for me to get a good head start?

It was all academic now, as I was out, and on the road.

The tree line started to look closer, but I realised after quite some time of walking that distances can be quite deceptive. Also, my fitness levels and stamina were very low after months of very little exercise. My initial burst of adrenaline had worn off and I felt extremely tired. I would have to stop. I found an area of rocks that I hoped would shield me from the road and fell into a restless sleep.

When I awoke, the sky was starting to darken and I realised that I had lost my advantage of meeting anyone that day, and would have to find somewhere sheltered for the night. Panic started to arise in me, but there was no alternative, so I started to do breathing exercises to help me calm down. The terrain looked so inhospitable, but not too far away was the start of the tree line. I reached it and found a small copse, into which I gratefully sank, just as darkness fell.

Pulling the padded jacket around me, I fell into a fretful sleep. Dark thoughts invaded my mind. I don't know what I was most afraid of, being eaten by some wild animal, or of him finding me. The morning came at last, and I must have had some refreshing sleep because I felt much more positive, and with some renewed hope. At least I had survived the night, though I wished I had kept the knife, just in case.

I would need to find some civilisation soon; I was hungry and thirsty. Under the cover of the trees, I walked slowly on.

Chapter Sixteen

Saved

The trees still afforded me a certain amount of shelter, so I walked on, keeping the road in my sights.

He must have recovered by now, so I would have to keep myself alert. I still didn't have any clear idea of where I was going, but surely the road must lead to somewhere. I reasoned that it must be mid-morning due to the position of the sun.

I started to feel very weak from hunger, but I knew I must continue on, hopefully in the right direction for Ásbyrgi. Later I heard the sound of a vehicle, so quickly hid in the scrubland at the side of the road.

A 4x4 car passed me and my heart almost stopped – could he have repaired his vehicle that quickly? It carried on down the road without reducing speed, so I reckoned that I had not been seen. I took deep breaths, trying to slow my racing heart rate, and thought that the car had more than one occupant, but perhaps I just imagined that.

However, it didn't mean it wasn't him. After some time I saw a track with a sign pointing towards Ásbyrgi.

My heart soared, but I wasn't safe yet, just right in my sense of direction. I finally reached a building that was the visitor's centre, but sadly it was closed, and there was no one around. I couldn't believe it. I stared and stared, willing someone to be there, but to no avail. I collapsed into a sobbing heap.

Once I had regained some control, I decided to have a proper look around the immediate area, peering firstly through the windows of the building, which appeared to be in two sections. An older wooden part and a newer glass section, which housed an exhibition space. The windows has pictures of birds etched into them, and I longed to be able to fly away and be free like them. The large door was locked. On one of the windows was a map, with instructions in both Icelandic and English, of a short walk down to a picnic area – Botnstjörn pond. Around the back of the building was a car park, with one vehicle parked – a red 4x4 family vehicle. Also, a signpost pointing to a narrow track between the trees, where I surmised that the car's occupants had gone. At least I hoped so.

I started down the track, bordered by birch and willow trees, and even some pines. Strange that I thought about trees, but my mind needed something normal to latch on to, rather than the horror of the past weeks. I hurried as best I could, but in my weakened state, it was really slow. I spent much of my time looking over my shoulder, afraid that he would jump out at me at any moment and take me back to the loft, where he would surely end my life. *Please, please, let me be saved.*

Finally, after a fraught, fear-ridden walk, I reached a clearing where ahead I could see an area with picnic tables, toilet facilities, and some sort of viewing platform overlooking a small lake. I could hear children's voices. A family were at one of the tables, with two children and a dog that ran at me, barking loudly. I was startled, as was the family. I had not taken into account my dishevelled appearance, especially just coming out of the trees like that. I could hear myself shouting, "Please help, please help, I am Anna, I was kidnapped, please help!" Blackness covered me and I hit the ground.

My opened my eyes to see a man leaning over me. I started to scream, then heard a woman's voice, comforting me. "Police," I said, "please get the police, he will come after me." In English they told me that they would drive me to the nearest police station. I was gratefully settled into the back of their car once back at the car park. I think the man must have carried me, but all I remember was being snuggled next to the dog.

Those poor children. I could hear myself ranting, "He has a black 4x4, he is dangerous, he kidnapped me." Then I must have lapsed into a very restless sleep, shouting out – I'm told – random bits of information. We arrived in a small town and I was taken to the police station. I tearfully thanked the man and woman and the children and said how sorry I was for scaring them. The man made his report to the police. In my bemused state, I could hear him speaking but not what he was saying as he had reverted to his native Icelandic. I waved across at him, and he smiled back.

I was taken to a room with a couch, given a hot drink, and offered food, of which I managed a little. I was told that a doctor had been called. A friendly policewoman had been assigned to sit with me. I was extremely nervous and reacted every time the door opened.

It was a very small police station, but I could hear much activity like talking and the ringing of phones. I fell into an exhausted sleep, perhaps helped by something the doctor gave me. I was told, on awakening, that a detective and forensic officers would be coming up from Reykjavik to see me. The doctor at the station had only given me a cursory examination, a more thorough one was to be done by the lady medical examiner. I agreed to everything. I was too traumatised to do anything else. I knew they would have to collect evidence, and of course any DNA from him that might still be on my person. He had raped me on many occasions. Shock must have set in, as I spent most of the time crying and shaking violently.

The team arrived from the capital and the ordeal of reliving everything began again.

Chapter Seventeen

Endless Questions

The medical examiner treated me with respect and although the examination was very intrusive, I knew she was there to help me.

Once I had settled, the detective and a female officer came to question me. At first, my mind had gone into complete lockdown, and I couldn't remember anything of the actual event, only arriving with my sister at the start of our holiday. I suppose I didn't want to remember the awful events that subsequently occurred.

They were very gentle and patient, asking me what seemed to be innocuous unrelated questions, and gradually I began to relax and remember small things. I knew there had been a storm and the police had closed off the roads. I remembered that because our coach driver was very annoyed – he was tired and wanted to get home to his family. He let me stay on the coach while the others went off to the cafe. I fell asleep then, and when I awoke, I was alone. It was very dark apart from the street lamps lighting the car park.

They listened carefully and I think I must have lapsed into periods of blankness, as I don't remember what

I said. The hospital doctor hovered nearby, saying at one point, that I really needed to be in the hospital at Reykjavik and that the questioning should continue there.

The male detective, though sympathetic, impressed on her that they needed details of the escape, especially the direction from which I had come, so they could continue their search for the car and the perpetrator. Apparently at the mention of the car I got very upset and agitated, repeating over and over, "I slashed the tyres, I slashed the tyres."

I was given a light sedative and the questions continued. How did I get to the picnic area? Where was I kept prisoner? I was shown a map of the area, but it meant nothing to me. I was only aware of the area around the hotel in Reykjavik. Everywhere else, we had been taken by coach. Perhaps some of the other people would know, or the driver, I can't have been on my own.

As to what happened in the car, I had no recollection, only of the strange hospital-type smell, which I later supposed to be chloroform.

They nodded at each other, then the doctor again voiced her objections more strongly, as I was clearly getting more and more upset. It was decided that they let me rest for a couple of hours. They did not waste the time, spending it organising a helicopter to take us all back to the capital. Also, apparently there was much liaison with the local police regarding isolated farms in the area, and owners of dark 4x4 vehicles, which was just about everyone.

When I woke again, I was asked if I could answer a few more questions before being transported back to a hospital in Reykjavik. The family who had helped me had been questioned, and they – the detectives – wanted to know my version of the events. I mumbled something about a track, then a road lined with scrubland and trees, then seeing a track with a signpost, which I decided to follow, but I didn't know why.

I remembered following the track and coming to a building with birds on the windows, and being upset because there was no one there. They asked me how I came to be at the pond area, but I didn't know. I did remember how relieved I felt when I saw the family. Next thing I knew, I was in a police station.

Again I was asked about the place where I was held, and became very agitated and tearful. I think my mind was trying to block it all out. It was decided that no further information would be forthcoming, so it would be of no further benefit to stay in this location.

I was told later it would be necessary for me to see a counsellor as well as the medical staff, as my mind had obviously put a block on everything related to the actual happenings at the place where I was held. I think I must have been sedated as I woke up in a large hospital, with many staff buzzing around me, a guard on the door, and no idea how I got there.

The detective and the female officer, who I was later told was also a detective, came to see me the following day. In my dreams, some of the details had started to come back, but I couldn't get past the tyre-slashing incident. When had that happened? Where was it? Who else was there? In my mind's eye, I could see a large space where a car was parked.

Many more questions were asked and with the help of the supportive people around me, I began to remember small details about the place, but not the events that took place there. When trying to remember the more sensitive details I would get upset and almost hysterical.

The police search for the location continued slowly, the whole area was very isolated with a number of small farms dotted around. I told them I could see horses from the place, and much barren countryside with snow-covered rocks strewn all around. I didn't know what sort of place I was in, my memory was confused with a sparse space with a ladder, and a room with more furniture, perhaps in a house. I couldn't make the distinction.

I was told that my family had been informed and were coming out to Iceland.

CHAPTER EIGHTEEN

Arrest

The nurses seemed very pleased by my progress and apart from my family not being there, the hospital experience was a good one.

I was treated well, the food was good, and I had been allowed up. However, the guard accompanied me if I left the ward for any reason. I wasn't very sure why that was.

Sadly, the reason became apparent some days later when the two detectives returned. I was now on first name terms with them. Gunnar and Agnes arrived with very serious-looking faces, and addressed me formally. I was perplexed.

They had asked for my doctor to be present also and again they went through the usual questions regarding the kidnap and the escape. On both counts, I could tell them no more than what had already been discussed. They spoke to each other in Icelandic then, to my utter amazement, the male detective cautioned me and arrested me for the murder of the man in the barn. Murder! All I knew was that I had slashed the tyres on the car that was hidden in the barn. I knew no more than that.

They were as sympathetic as they could be. I became more and more agitated and the doctor must have intervened and given me a sedative because I remembered no more. Once I was awake again, there was a police woman by my bedside, and the doctor was called. I didn't know what was going on until the police woman explained that I was actually under arrest, and awaiting removal to a prison hospital to await trial.

How could I be under arrest; I was the victim, wasn't I? I was told nicely but firmly that I would be accompanied everywhere I went, including the toilets, until my case came to trial. I was also to be put on suicide watch. I was horrified, as was my doctor and the nursing team. I could hear the doctor arguing with the detectives, although I didn't know what they were saying. I was told I would have an interpreter assigned to me, and also that the British Embassy in Reykjavik would be informed, as was procedure when any foreign nationals were arrested.

I cried, "How can this be?" I had tried so hard to escape from the nightmare, and now I was right back in it. They told me that my family had been informed of my escape, and that they would be coming back to Iceland to see me. They being my husband, Michael, and sister, Christina. At least that was something to be happy about; it would be wonderful to see some truly friendly faces.

The nursing staff were still as caring and friendly – I suspect that they felt sorry for the way things were turning out – but the atmosphere in the room had changed. They were no longer allowed to make any reference to what had happened, not that I had much to tell them, my memory was still very patchy to say the least. What had happened when, and in what order, I had no idea. It made me feel very isolated, I never felt so utterly alone.

I was assigned a team of lawyers; two females came to see me and took notes at my bedside. They told me that the more in-depth interviews would take place once I was moved to the holding prison hospital. It was so surreal. In my sleeping hours, chemically induced by sleeping pills, I would be at home with Michael, and all of this was a bad dream. However, a dream it was not, and the nightmare went on.

On the day before my family arrived, I was formally charged, my rights read out to me in English and Icelandic, and the interpreter was also there to clarify any language points I did not understand. I was also made ready to be moved to the more secure prison location. I knew that the word 'murder' had been used, but I couldn't equate that with the destroying of property. It all seemed to be unnecessarily severe.

My depression deepened and apparently I shouted out in my sleep about tyres and slashing. My family members arrived, brought to the prison from the airport. They were given a briefing by the detectives. They were absolutely horrified and Christina was incensed that I should be charged with such a crime. My poor Michael apparently was just too shocked to say anything. He had had enough problems getting his mind to accept what had happened to me in the first place, and now there was this atrocity to deal with. When they were allowed to see me, Christina was very comforting, and tried to talk about more mundane things happening at home. She spoke about our boys, Martin and Paul, and Mum and Dad. She told me about Paul previously coming out to Iceland, and him helping in the search.

It was all too awful and I couldn't really take it all in. Why couldn't I remember? A psychologist had been sent to see me, and he explained that it was a way of the mind healing itself, and trying to make sense of all that had happened. I just wanted it all to go away.

The British Embassy had been informed, as was the normal protocol, and two members of the consulate were allowed ongoing visits with me and were kept informed of all aspects of the case.

A court date was fixed quite quickly, as was the norm for the Icelandic judicial system, and I would have to appear for the arraignment. It would be a district court, before a panel of judges. My family members had decided to stay on in Iceland as this was to take place within days.

What sort of nightmare was that going to be? I couldn't bear the thought of it and once again everything started to close down and I spent much of the time sedated.

PART TWO

CHRISTINA'S STORY

CHAPTER NINETEEN

First Alerts

"You haven't seen my sister, have you?"

"No," was the reply from everyone.

I started to feel uneasy, the wind had abated a little, and our coach driver had come into the cafe. I asked him about Anna, to which he replied that there was no one left on the coach. He had heard the doors open and close and presumed that she had come over to the cafe.

The cafe itself covered a large area, with many people from the various coaches milling about, so I wasn't too worried. There were also a number of small shops on the complex, and of course, the toilet areas.

After more than half an hour, the nagging little doubts and worries started to multiply. Surely she would have come to look for me. I went to see our guide and told her of my fears. The cafe had a sort of tannoy system, so she asked for an announcement to be made for Anna to come to the exit doors where we would meet her. After twenty minutes and a no-show, I started to panic.

The storm had started to die down a little, but it was still raining – a sort of sleet-laden rain. The guide went to see some of the other coach drivers, and a call went out for volunteers to make a search party of the complex in case she had fallen somewhere.

A large number of people volunteered which both surprised and heartened me. We searched, but to no avail. The coach drivers each went back to their coaches to see if perhaps she had got back onto the wrong coach and gone back to sleep. This also drew a blank.

A discussion went on between the other guides and the drivers, and it was decided to inform the police. This would probably take some time as most were out already, manning the road blocks of the closed off roads.

The happy, noisy atmosphere in the cafe slowly quietened down to agitated whispers around the tables. I could not rest; my mind had gone into overdrive, full of 'what if' scenarios. Our guide sat with me and did her best to keep me calm and positive.

Time almost seems to go backwards when you are waiting for something to happen, and after what seemed like an eternity, two police cars arrived. Everyone was asked to stay at their tables, then they were divided into those who were tourists, and those locals on their way home.

The police, two teams of one man and one woman, began a systematic sweep of each table. Of course, the passengers from the other coaches had no idea who Anna was, nor what she looked like, so I provided what photographs I had. This process went on for quite some time.

The storm had by now abated and people were getting anxious about getting home, or back to their hotels. The police took information from each coach driver about their itinerary and passenger lists, where they were staying, and any information they could glean. One by one people were allowed to leave, our coach passengers being the last ones. The local people had to account for their movements prior to and arriving at the cafe, and their addresses taken. They, like us, had mostly been directed there by the police because of the storm.

The cafe did have CCTV but due to the adverse conditions, the images were very dark and blurred. Three vehicles could be seen to be leaving during the time period, but sadly it was only an unclear image of their shape, and no definite details.

I was hysterical by this time. *Where could she be?* Naturally, my mind went to the worst possible scenario, so I tried very hard to keep such negative thoughts under control.

Anna's handbag and camera had been recovered from the coach and taken as evidence. I was taken back to Reykjavik in a police vehicle to the hotel where a police woman was designated to stay with me until the morning.

I was told that a detailed search of the cafe and surrounds would be conducted in the daylight, as stumbling about in the dark would not be of any help to the investigation. Iceland had a very low serious crime rate, but there had been a kidnap case a few years earlier where a young woman had disappeared and been found murdered. Following that, security had been stepped up and CCTV placed in many new areas; however, they were still not so well equipped like British or American cities. It was, I was told, extremely unusual for a tourist to go missing. I tried to let that be of comfort to me, but failed miserably.

I had decided not to phone the families back home, as this was still early on, and could hopefully still be resolved in a positive way. I didn't want to worry people unnecessarily, however, the burden of it was becoming overwhelming.

Why didn't I make her get off the coach with me? Why didn't I go and check on her? Could I have done anything to help or stop situation? What happened to her while I was in the cafe, warm, drinking coffee, and chatting with the other passengers? I felt the questions would drive me mad.

There was a knock on the door. I rushed to open it, thinking it would be some news. My police woman had gone to breakfast, I, however, had no appetite. It was one of the other coach passengers Anna and I had chatted with. She had come to see if she could help in any way. I burst into a flood of tears, and she sat, arms around my shoulders, listening to my sobs. Later she brought me a hot drink and a small snack laid on by the kitchen and persuaded me to eat at least a little.

Later my police woman came back and we all went down to the lounge area where I was told of enquiries thus far.

CHAPTER TWENTY

The Police

The police from the previous evening arrived. One of the teams, plus a plain-clothes person I took to be a detective. I was taken to a quiet area used only by the hotel staff.

They had come from the HQ at Laugavegur, essentially to check on the details of my story. It was not unknown for siblings to fall out and do each other damage. I was too upset to be offended.

Teams of tracker dogs had been sent to the cafe location and the petrol station, and were searching using the scent from Anna's handbag and contents. I had pretty much descended into a world of my own, too shocked to face the reality of the situation. I became fixated by the name on the back of their uniform jackets – 'Logregian' – which I later found out meant 'law order'. Sadly, I wasn't of much help and answered their questions with a certain air of detachment.

I wanted to fill my mind with more mundane matters, like getting home, telling the family, and sorting time off from my employment. I desperately wanted my sister to walk back into the hotel, laughing and telling me about what an adventure she'd had.

The police woman's voice cut through my reverie and brought me back to the present situation with a bump. I started to cry. They – the police – were sympathetic, but also very dogged in their questioning. They obviously wanted to solve this mystery as quickly as possible, and I realised it was natural that they would think of me as a suspect. However, I wasn't under arrest, but it was made very clear that I needed to co-operate.

I had asked for someone to be with me, and the caring lady, Karen, was sent for to be of comfort to me, and also as an independent witness during any interrogation. She happily complied, and sat holding my hand during the rest of the proceedings. The detective, a man named Erik – nice enough in his way, a little gruff, but efficient – asked me many probing questions. Mainly about my relationship with my sister and said that others on the coach had heard us arguing. "Oh that," I said, "we often argue, nothing serious, it's just that she is always wanting to be early for things, and my tardiness makes her annoyed."

"Tardiness? What do you mean?"

"Sorry, I mean that I am always late – according to her – and we argue about it. It is not serious; we have been doing it since we were children. Just differences in personality." That seemed to satisfy them.

They told me that they had asked for an article to be placed into the *Fettablaoio* newspaper, and asked if

I could provide some pictures. I readily agreed. Also, they had been in touch with the National Broadcasting Service, RÚV, to ask for any information to be reported to the nearest police station. I could not fault them; they were taking the whole incident very seriously.

A mention was made, in passing, about the previous kidnap case, but at the time I didn't know the significance of that. At the cafe site, the red and blue uniformed ICE-SAR had been called out to investigate the car park and surrounding area. This was the Icelandic Association for Search and Rescue, and was made up of well-trained emergency response volunteers. I was told that the search would go on for several days or until a conclusion was reached, and it was up to me if I stayed or not. In Iceland or at home, I would, of course, be kept informed of any updates.

I eventually phoned home and told the families the news. I decided to stay on for another four days, making arrangements with my husband, the hotel, and changing mine and my sister's flight. Anna's son was due to fly over as soon as he could make any necessary arrangements. There was nothing else any of us could do.

I felt absolutely numb and went through the making of the new plans like a zombie. I was very grateful for Karen's help. She and her husband, Rob, were of very great comfort to me. I had asked my husband to stay at home with the children, and told him that I was being very well looked after.

The police had arranged for me to see a local doctor who prescribed pills to help me sleep and keep me calm.

Karen was still there for a couple of days, but I felt bad about spoiling her holiday and begged her to continue with her plans. We came to a compromise – she and her husband would go on their trips in the day, and would sit with me in the evening when the darkest clouds of worry and sadness would come over me. The hotel people were very sympathetic, and the police would visit me at various times.

My days went by very slowly and there was still no news as such. Sadly the wind and the rain had washed away much of the evidence, if indeed there had been any at the scene. However, due to the broadcasts on the radio, two of the car drivers had come forward and been cleared from the police enquiries.

The CCTV recordings of the night had been meticulously studied and a lone, figure-shaped shadow – thought to be Anna – could be seen by a lamppost, and a large black vehicle shape could be seen pulling up. After that there was no clear vision of anything as the storm had reached its height at that point and obliterated any images by blowing the camera to a slightly new angle. The recordings from the petrol station were no better. The rest of the night's images just showed the movement of the searchers, but again, in no detail.

I was in despair, my dearly loved sister had just vanished in the wind and into who knew what sort of nightmare.

Chapter Twenty-one

Support from Home

The police kept me well informed. The rest of the coach party left for their return trip to England. My solace in all of this, Karen, also left.

Anna's son, Paul, thankfully a mature young man of 22, was due to fly in midmorning. The police said they wanted to take me back to the cafe location and go again through all of the details. I readily agreed. I had been through the scenario in my every moment, waking and sleeping, but asked if we could wait until Paul arrived as he was anxious to learn everything he could. The police agreed.

They took me to the airport to meet him, and brought us back to the hotel for some food. I could see how shocked and worried he was, so eating was the last thing on our minds.

The car drove out to the location early afternoon while there was still some daylight. It had been very dark, with a fierce storm raging when I had last been there. Consequently, I didn't recognize anything except the cafe. Paul was very quiet. We sat in the back of the car not speaking, but with him holding my hand. He was my nephew, but I loved him like my own.

The cafe had been closed for a few days while the police forensic team had been working there. Now parts of it were open, but the rest and part of the car park were still cordoned off. Sadly, little had been found due to the high winds and torrential sleet and rain from the night in question.

We walked to the cafe, where I went over my every move, from leaving the coach, my seat in the cafe, who I spoke to, and my general impressions of the night. I was asked if I had noticed any people on their own, but the answer was no – I was too busy chatting with my fellow passengers, and drinking the warming coffee.

Paul said nothing and although he looked calm, I knew he wasn't. When he was agitated his right leg would be in constant movement, a nervous condition he had had since a child. I felt so sorry for him, I knew how worried I was, and he must have been feeling it even more. After all, it was his mother who was missing.

We walked around the car park, past the lamppost where the blurry figure had been seen. The road was clear and everything that might have been of use, like tyre tracks, had been washed away. We went to where I thought the coach had been parked, and from there followed my route back to the cafe.

There were a few customers in there, not at all surprised to see the police. There had been a number of news bulletins, and as the cafe was not yet back as a coach stop, presumably the people there were locals. One member of the forensics team came in and sat with us, ostensibly to discuss the outer areas. But we found out later that the man was a 'profiler', paying particular attention to the people gathered there. The perpetrators of crimes would often return to the scene, or put themselves forward to help with the investigation, so they would know of any breakthroughs.

He casually asked if I recognised anyone, but I was too traumatized to think of anything. Most of the conversation was in Icelandic, with the odd explanation thrown our way. At last. we went back to the hotel.

A meeting was scheduled for early evening, mainly to give Paul a chance to rest and talk with me. Once the police left, we hugged each other and wept. We both feared the worst, even though we didn't speak it out loud.

The evening came and it was decided that we should have the meeting at the police station, mainly for privacy reasons. A police car picked us up and we made our way, in silence, to the station. There had been a new light covering of snow on the higher areas of the city, and it was so cold, but nothing that matched the cold fear in my heart.

We were taken to a large office; in there were several officers, including some plain-clothes officers and a high-ranking female who was obviously leading the investigation. She spoke first and assured us that they were doing everything possible, but sadly, as yet, there were no leads apart from the blurry images on the CCTV footage. Unfortunately, the loss of any detail had prevented any definite identification of the third vehicle, the other two having already been eliminated from the enquiry.

All they could do at present was to continue with their questions and searches, which would now include looking back at many days of CCTV in and around the cafe to see if they could find a pattern of behaviour in any of the customers.

Paul and I listened but I have to say I was completely numb; it was like hearing the plot for a film. My mind had just shut down; I felt detached and couldn't shake off the overriding foreboding of tragedy. Paul asked some questions, but I didn't really take in what was said. The meeting finished with a promise to continue the investigation, and a suggestion that Paul and I return home to England until there was actually some news.

It was with great sadness that two days later I boarded a plane home. Paul had decided to stay for a few more days, with a promise to phone me each day with updates. I would have to do my best to settle back into my life, with the love and support of my family around me.

How to do this, when I felt so responsible.

CHAPTER TWENTY-TWO

Home again

The plane touched down, I disembarked and walked down to the baggage hall in a daze. I just couldn't believe what had happened and what was still happening. My suitcase retrieved, I walked through to customs control. I think they must have been alerted because a kindly female customs officer came forward to help me. She muttered something about being very sorry, then guided me through to a side exit where Adam and my son, Martin, were waiting. In my husband's arms I sobbed, the floodgates now fully opened.

He lead me to our car and we rode home pretty much in silence apart from my sobs. I told him that I just couldn't believe it. It was as if Anna had been spirited away from the face of the earth. I felt so responsible, and yet I knew it was not my fault. Adam gently told me that I must not blame myself; it had been a series of circumstances that had led up to her disappearance. No amount of me going over and over the details was going to make the outcome any different. He had such a calm demeanour and I loved him for it. Martin, poor lad, didn't really know what to say, so I told him to go off to his girlfriend's house as he would do normally.

We made the dreaded phone call to Anna's house, to say I was back home and made arrangements to meet up with her partner, Michael, that evening.

I slept most of the rest of the day. Adam prepared our meal and insisted that I ate at least something, then it was time to go off to see Michael. The house was quiet and dark-looking when we pulled up outside. The door was answered by our mother, who, with Father, had been sitting in the semi-dark with Michael. They were all waiting to hear what details I could give them.

Adam sat close to me as I retold the story, some of which they knew as it had made the BBC news site on the internet. They desperately wanted to hear my version of it. They wanted to know all about it, including our time leading up to the disappearance. With a shaking voice, I told them about the trip from the beginning. About looking for the whales, even managing a smile as I described the other passengers looking like polar bears in their snow-covered coats. I stopped. Were they sure they wanted to hear all of this? But they urged me to carry on. Perhaps they needed to know that Anna had been happy before events overtook her. I told them about luxuriating in the warm springs at the Blue Lagoon, and about the amazing geysers, and about sitting in a field awaiting the appearance of the aurora, which, of course, didn't happen.

I started to tell them about the Golden Circle trip, and this was where I broke down. The memory was still so very raw.

A hot toddy later, I was able to go on. The day had started well, and although there had been some weather warnings, it was decided the trip would go ahead. The coach was full of other passengers, mostly from our hotel, but with some other pickups around the city. We were driven out to the tectonic plates area, where Anna and I had gone off taking photographs and meeting in the small cafe area.

Once everyone was back on board the coach we were taken around the area, the guide filling in general and geological information. The wind had started to pick up, and the heavy sleet-type rain had started. The weather had worsened, and in a very short time, it had become very dark and visibility was very much affected.

At one of the crossroads there was a police roadblock, and we, along with all other traffic, were directed to a cafe area atop one of the hills. There was a large car park with enough space to accommodate many vehicles. On our arrival, we were directed into the cafe. Anna had begun to feel – unusually for her – a little travelsick and decided to stay on the coach to sleep it off. I went into the cafe with the other passengers. It was warm and there was plenty of food and drinks, and a noisy friendly atmosphere. Our coach people mostly sat together, chatting and getting to know each other more.

I wasn't sure how long we had been in there when I realised I hadn't seen Anna. I was sure she would have awoken by then, she was known for her short 'cat naps'. The coach driver came into the cafe, and when asked, told me there was no one left on the coach. I went to see our guide, and she and I, with a few of the other passengers, searched the cafe and the small shops on the complex. We didn't go outside at that point as the storm was still raging. The coach driver said he had seen no one on his way over to the cafe. After an announcement was made on the tannoy system, and she was still a no-show, it was decided to call in the police. Two squad cars arrived and a search was made of the car park and the other coaches. She was nowhere to be found.

At this point I broke down.

Once recovered, I told them about the police involvement, and what steps had been thus far taken. Also about the newspaper article and the radio broadcast, and the work of the forensic teams. I told them too about my interviews, the help of the lovely lady, Karen, and the arrival of Paul. I assured them that the police could not have been more helpful.

This was all I could tell them. I reluctantly came home with a promise from the police to keep everyone informed of any updates. There was silence throughout; I think everyone was just too stunned to take in the information.

After a couple of hours, Adam and I went home and I was awake most of the night, reliving the whole terrible episode.

CHAPTER TWENTY-THREE

Paul's Return

Paul had decided to stay out in Iceland for a few more days following my return home.

The police had been very busy those first days checking out footage from around the area of the cafe. Sadly, there was very little to act on as the storm had affected most of the cameras that were in operation and what images there were, were very unclear.

They were also following up leads phoned in by members of the public after the newspaper, radio, and TV appeals. They were still looking for the third vehicle that had left the car park, having already eliminated the other two drivers. Each of the coach drivers had also been questioned, but no one had seen anything.

Paul was there mainly to give what information he could about his mother, including a detailed description. He told us, on his return, how helpless he felt but that he was impressed by the police response, how they had prioritised the case, and allotted a great many resources to it. I know all of this because he came to see my husband and I once he was home. We commiserated with each other, and each spoke of our feelings of abandonment of Anna. Naturally, we could not stay in Iceland long-term, and would probably have become a hindrance to the police. They had promised to keep us updated on all developments.

I felt that Paul should be at home to support his father, who had gone into a state of stasis, and also to try to carry out some semblance of a normal life, if at all possible. I had Adam and Martin to help me, and also there was Mum and Dad.

How could such an anticipated and enjoyed – to a point – holiday have gone so wrong, and with such serious consequences? My poor Anna. I cried every time I thought about it.

The case had also been reported in our national press, but as yet Scotland Yard had not been called upon to assist. I was signed off work by my GP for at least three weeks. Everyone was very understanding. Snippets of news were passed on to us, but there had been no substantial breakthrough. I couldn't bear it. My instinct was to go back to Iceland to search myself, but I realised that it was futile; the police and the specialised teams were doing all they could.

Paul told me they had mounted a massive vehicle search, but most vehicles were dark 4x4s, so to pinpoint the one on the CCTV was almost impossible unless the driver came forward of his or her own volition, and as yet that hadn't happened. There was very little evidence of any kind; the tracker dogs had come up with nothing. The storm had been very efficient in wiping everything clean.

Each week we waited, but as time went by we began to lose hope and the dreadful thought that she might already be dead came and stayed in our minds. Adam suggested that I go for counselling and this was arranged through our local GP. I felt so responsible and couldn't shake the idea.

We had a few false alarms – leads that went nowhere – and it seemed like the investigation was being downgraded. Adam and I decided that we would travel back to Iceland for a few days and make some enquiries of our own. We hired a car and visited the cafe area.

Adam was shocked to see how remote it was, and with that coupled with my description of the dreadful storm, he began to see how hopeless it all was. We went into the cafe and through the ordeal of asking questions, but to no avail; the staff there didn't know any more than they had already told the police.

We also visited the Reykjavik police HQ where we were treated respectfully, but also firmly told that they were doing all they could and would let us know of any further developments. We returned home.

Once home again, we had a family conference with Michael, Paul, Mum, and Dad. Martin had gone back to university, trying to continue with his normal life. With great sadness, we all decided that we had to continue with our everyday lives until there was any news. It could take years, or perhaps never at all, but we still all carried that faint flicker of hope in our hearts.

We decided to hold a form of memorial service at our house, inviting friends and family. We made it very clear that it was not a wake but a remembrance – a form of closure for at least this part of the proceedings. It was important to be able to speak about Anna, and not pretend it wasn't happening. It turned out to be a joyful occasion, everyone dealing with the situation in their own way. Again and again, it was stressed this was not to imply she had died, but to celebrate what we knew of her until we had any news to the contrary. It was comforting in a strange way, and made me feel nearer to my sister, and assuaged some of the guilt I felt for not insisting that she came to the cafe with the rest of the passengers.

Speaking of passengers, some of them had kept in touch via a WhatsApp group where information could be shared very quickly. People had been very kind. After a while, it all seemed to be unreal, like we were speaking about one of the 'Scandi noir' dramas on the TV, except this time it was real.

Several months passed.

Chapter Twenty-four

News at Last

One evening in early May we received a phone call from Michael. The Icelandic police had been in touch and we were asked to travel back there.

We were overjoyed but something in Michael's tone told us all was not well. We, that's Michael, Adam and I, booked flights for the following day. We asked our boys to stay at home for the present. The police met us at the airport and escorted us to the HQ building where we were told all of our questions would be answered. We spent a very nervous journey in the car, convinced they were going to tell us Anna had been found dead.

The station was busy and we were shown into a side room, given hot drinks, and asked to wait patiently for the two detectives who had been assigned to the case. Very stoic people, they gave nothing away with their facial expressions, and we were too bemused to do anything but what they asked.

Paul had also wanted to come, but his father had asked him to stay at home and make any arrangements that may be necessary. The door opened and the detectives came in. We immediately bombarded them with questions. We were assured that she was not dead, however, there were several problems.

The female officer took over the speaking. She – Anna that is – had managed to escape her captor and was rescued by a family who had taken her to the local police station. This had taken place many miles away, in the north east of the country, in the Vatnajökull National Park area, which they pinpointed on a large wall map for us. I was stunned; it was so far away from where we had last been. No wonder she couldn't be found.

The police woman's voice brought me back to the room. There was, she said, a problem. Details of the abduction and the holding of her captive seemed to have been wiped from her memory. She had gone into a form of posttraumatic trauma shock; they didn't know how long it would last, or if it would be permanent or not. Sadly, there was an added complication. When the police had finally found where she was being held, they made another discovery. A man's body.

Anna could not account for that, and kept repeating that she slashed the tyres on the vehicle whilst making her escape so he could not follow her. We were all shocked. Was she hurt? Where was she?

She was in hospital, under guard – for her protection as much as anything else as there may have been an accomplice. More enquiries needed to be made. Under guard! Every time something was said, the situation was much worse. We were to be taken to the hospital, and asked to prepare ourselves for what we would see. Michael said absolutely nothing, his expression blank, and I felt the floor starting to slide away from me and only the grip of my husband's hand and his comforting voice stopped me from fainting.

At the hospital we were taken to a quiet side ward where Anna had been kept pretty much under sedation as in her waking periods she would cry out if any male staff members went anywhere near her, and all she spoke about were the tyres. When we saw her, it was hard to recognize this thin creature in the bed as my sister. She had lost a lot of weight, and had a pallor giving her a ghostly appearance. How could this be my vibrant, adventurous sister? I just broke down and sobbed. The two men just stared.

I thought there was a little semblance of recognition, but it was hard to tell. There were nurses assigned to her 24 hours a day, and we were told she was getting good care. There was no point in staying as she was sedated, but we would be informed as soon as she was awake.

We were escorted back to the police station and told more of the story.

The police enquiries had been ongoing since the night of the incident. I was again asked to give another statement in case I had remembered anything else. This was of no help as I was in the cafe during the whole episode and saw nothing until the searchers arrived. The feelings of guilt flooded back to me. *Why didn't I know she was in trouble? Could I have done more?* Adam sensed my turmoil, and sat down, his protective arms around me. Michael just seemed as if he had gone into his own silent world. I wondered if he blamed me for what had happened. I wouldn't have been surprised, even I blamed me.

So, how had they found the person responsible? The police up in the northern parts of the country had also been alerted, and the search had been carried out countrywide. Using the snippets of information they had, they reckoned that on her escape, she couldn't have travelled too far from where she was kept, given her poor state. At first she had been able to give some information, but as they delved deeper into the account, she started to go into delayed shock, finally muttering incoherently about slashing tyres. After that, there was nothing but garbled words.

A map had been obtained, highlighting the many isolated farms in the region, especially those where there were horses, and could be reached by all-terrain vehicles. Also there was the continuing search for the 4x4 seen leaving the cafe car park. All farms had to be visited and eliminated from the enquiries. It had not been expected that a kidnap victim would be taken so far away from the original pick-up point. Had she gone willingly? That would never really be known, but I answered most strongly that she must have been knocked out – she had a husband and son at home whom she loved dearly. Also, the fact that she escaped was surely a testament to her desire to return home.

Finally, the right farm had been located and approached stealthily by the police and members of the ICE-SAR team. All were armed as it wasn't known if the occupants had an arsenal of weapons at their disposal. As they neared the house a dog started barking, but after five minutes, with no sign of life, they entered the house, and the large barn next to it. The house was clear of anyone; half-eaten food was on the table, and many empty whisky bottles.

The barn was approached very carefully. Parked inside was a black 4x4 vehicle, and a vertical ladder leading up to a makeshift room, the door of which was open. Some of the team went up to investigate. Inside they could see a makeshift bed, some rope bindings and remnants of food. A shout went up from a member searching the downstairs part of the barn. A body had been found. The man was obviously dead, so the forensics team were called and the area cordoned off.

OMG. What had gone on there? The police continued their story. There were two scenes of interest – the upstairs room where many items were bagged up to be investigated back at the forensic laboratory, and also the area around the body. The man had injuries that were synonymous with a fall from a height – a head injury – but it would not have killed him, just knocked him out. The body smelt of alcohol. What had killed him were the stab wounds slashed across his body. There was no weapon present, but they would continue to search for that. Oh my poor Anna, what had happened there? She constantly raved about the tyres being slashed but apparently they weren't, so we could only surmise that in her terrified mind she had confused him for the vehicle.

CHAPTER TWENTY-FIVE

Court Case

The case was to go to the heraosdomstolar, the district court, a few days hence. We all decided to attend. Adam, Martin, and I, Michael, and Paul. Mum and Dad had flown home having said their goodbyes to Anna, they just couldn't bear the stress of it all. Besides being support for Anna, we realised that Michael was in a really bad way, and also needed our help.

The court set-up was very different to what we were used to, or expected. There was no jury, just a bench of three judges who heard the evidence, then decided on the appropriate punishment. There was a court of appeal should that be needed.

Anna's case was unique in many respects. Firstly, she was a foreign national, she had been the victim of a kidnapping and multiple rapes, also she had no recollection of certain aspects of the incidents in question. But the undisputed fact was that there had been a killing and Anna was the prime suspect.

She sat impassively throughout the giving of the prosecution's evidence, her pale face showing no emotion until it came to the part about the vehicle and the alleged slashing of the tyres. The prosecution maintained that the tyres were actually intact, and at this point Anna became very unsettled and called out. She was asked nicely but firmly to remain silent until it was the turn of the defence lawyers. She was so obviously upset, and my heart went out to her. I just wanted to rush up and hug her. She looked so vulnerable up there on her own, nothing like the strong, adventurous Anna that I knew.

Various witnesses were called, mainly from the search and rescue team who had found the body, but, as yet, not the weapon. They described the storming of the barn, finding the dark 4x4 vehicle parked inside, and the finding of the body. Forensics had been called, and the whole area sectioned off. Anna had been at the local police station, then the hospital, for all of that time, having been rescued by the family at the picnic site.

We all sat listening to the proceedings, the information being relayed to us in English by an interpreter. She had been given legal aid under Article 126 Act of Civil Procedure 91/1991, and a defence team allocated. When it was their turn they argued that Anna had been subjected to the most awful ordeal, and went on to describe what they knew to have happened. Anything else was, of course, conjecture.

Then it was time for Anna to give her evidence. Her memories were very patchy, and also she could make no distinction of what had happened, and when. She said she had been seen in the small hospital by the medical examiner, and also been seen by two psychologists – all of whom were to be called as witnesses, she believed. Other than that, she had no recollection.

The medical examiner was called and told the court that Anna had been examined for evidence of sexual abuse, which was confirmed. The psychologists also gave their findings, agreeing that they thought that Anna suffered from confabulation as part of her breakdown.

What on earth was that? We had never heard of such a thing. Apparently it was a condition – a memory error – in which a person confused imagined or made-up scenarios with actual memories. In Anna's mind she had slashed the car tyres, and nothing could sway her away from that belief. But it had been shown in the prosecution's case that the tyres were intact.

It was certainly a conundrum. A crime had been committed; a man was dead, slashed in a frenzied attack. But was Anna truly culpable following her dreadful ordeal? Was it planned, was it opportunistic, or even self-defence? What had really happened in that barn? Who would ever really know? In her more lucid moments, Anna had muttered something about a ladder to the loft, and that it was dangerous and that the man had fallen, she thought. He was often in a state of drunkenness. She thought he had banged his head.

Around the barn were various farm implements and a workbench of sorts. It was there, she said, she found the tool to slash the tyres. All she remembered after that was taking the work coat from a hook by the door, and getting away as fast as she could, before he woke up.

She remembered going down a track, and coming to a road, where she randomly turned one way. Each time she heard a vehicle she hid in the undergrowth at the side of the road. Anna was asked about the knife. She said she didn't really know what the tool had been and she couldn't remember where she dropped it, it must have been in the barn. But this wasn't so, as it had not been found by the search team. Already greatly upset by this point, her agitation grew stronger and a break was asked for, and granted.

We, her family, were all so worried. There was no concrete evidence either way, no weapon, but no matter what, the man was still dead and Anna had been the only one there. What was still very unclear were his motives for abducting her in the first place. He had at one point been married, but his wife had gone off with his brother to settle in Canada. Perhaps it was that, that had tipped him over the edge.

The judges retired to make their deliberations, and on their return gave their verdict. Murder was a very serious crime, and the evidence did point to a guilty verdict as there was evidence of Anna's presence. But given all the extenuating circumstances, she was found guilty but with diminished responsibility and given the lightest sentence available – a maximum of four years. This was to be served mainly in the prison hospital wing.

We were horrified, but the lawyers told us not to despair as we could take it to the appeal court, but as it was such a unique case, it was unlikely that the full term would be served. Also, we could apply to have the sentence carried out in the UK where her family would be nearer. The lawyers said they would help with the appropriate paperwork.

Adam took charge and he and Martin immediately started proceedings. First, they would need to receive the form for rights and options, which needed all the necessary signatures, including Anna's and Michael's. They also read up on the terms and conditions of the Council of Europe Convention on the Transfer of Sentenced Persons.

I was too upset to function properly – it had brought back all the guilty feelings of abandoning her at the coach park. Michael was just too stunned to function well, so Paul spent his time looking after his father. Poor Michael. What a dreadful situation, what must be going through his head? Fortunately, Paul was very level-headed and took over straight away. What were we to say to Mum and Dad?

The last we saw of Anna was when she looked across at us and lifted her hand in a half-wave. Behind her eyes, there was nothing.

She was returned to the hospital wing.

Chapter Twenty-six

Transfer to UK

We all returned home, shell-shocked. Adam and I had the awful task of going to tell Mum and Dad the latest news. Michael was in no fit state.

We all felt it should have been a suspended sentence, but the fact was it was classed as a murder, and as such deserved a fitting sentence. There was no definitive explanation as to what had gone on in that barn. Anna had no defensive wounds so it could not be construed as self-defence, and the final outcome was that a man was dead, whatever the circumstances.

My nightmares returned, but I was able to take some solace from my counselling sessions. The feelings of guilt were even more acute now. Poor, poor, Anna.

We had been told that it would take some time to arrange the transfer to an English prison, which would also need to have access to a hospital wing. Anna would need to be under the care of a psychiatrist, and probably with psychologists involved. We petitioned for her to be placed in Voston Hall, a closed women's prison, which would be easier for us to visit, whilst still fulfilling the terms of her sentence. We all felt that she needed all the support we could give her. It was all too awful, that a holiday could have such dire and far-reaching consequences. It was not just Anna – it had affected the whole family, especially Michael and Paul.

It had been reported in the national press and at first we had been plagued by reporters wanting to know the story details. These we weren't able to give, as we didn't really know. Only Anna knew, and all the details of the incidences had become locked in her mind. After a while, a new story broke and they left us alone. Paul had kept them away from Michael, who had suffered a nervous breakdown. He had never been a strong man, Anna was definitely the one of strength in the marriage, and he was lost without her. Also, what he privately thought of it all, he didn't tell us.

Every few weeks a member of the family would go out to visit Anna in Iceland. I came to dread it when it was my turn, I really didn't know what to say to her. It had been suggested by her carers that we just speak of mundane everyday matters, but to alert the staff if she started to remember any details. What a truly awful situation.

The transfer took a couple of months to arrange but finally things started to come together, such as the necessary documentation and escort details. Prisoners had to pay for their own airline tickets, plus any other transport details. The family all contributed to the costs. We were surprised that it would be a normal flight, but Anna was not deemed to be of a danger to the general public and, of course, the escort would be present in the event of any trouble.

All we wanted was to get her back to the UK, and continue our lives as best we could.

Once she was installed in her new place of incarceration, we would be given visiting details. It was a very anxious few months but finally the news came through that she had been successfully moved. We waited patiently for our visiting rights.

She had been allowed to go to Voston Hall, Derbyshire, which, in travelling time, was thankfully quite near to our homes. On my first visit I was very worked up, still plagued by my guilty feelings. The counselling was helping, but I had still not come to terms with it all. Such dire occurrences always affect more than just the victim, and we as a family were still struggling with everything.

To my surprise, she looked really well and pleased to see me. I had expected to see the pale, haunted-looking creature I had last seen in Iceland, but she looked so much better. Our conversation was at first a little stilted, but after a few visits we fell into our old way of chatter. I had been told not to question her on any of the happenings unless she brought it up first, and then to report it to the staff. Consequently, our first few visits were solely about family.

Paul had gone with Michael, but it was he who had done all of the talking. Michael had not fully recovered from his breakdown, although there must have been many questions in his head. We had all been as supportive as we could, especially Adam, as I felt that my presence upset Michael and that he in some ways blamed me for what had happened. Rightly or wrongly, it was how I felt too.

Anna steadily recovered, looking better each time I went to visit, for which I was thankful. During her second year there we were told there was to be a review of her case, with a chance of a parole hearing, which – if successful – would allow her out on licence.

Naturally, all of this would take some time, but we were hopeful. She would, on the very rare occasion, talk about our Icelandic holiday, but only about the trips; there was never any mention of what had happened after she disappeared. I wondered if she would ever be able to speak of the awful events ever again.

On one of my visits, I was asked to see one of the doctors. I was greatly alarmed, fearing that there had been a relapse, but it was just to inform me that a parole hearing had been scheduled. We, the family, would be informed of the details nearer the date. There was no guarantee that she would be released, but it was a good start towards her coming home.

CHAPTER TWENTY-SEVEN

Revelations

The parole hearing had been arranged and Michael and I were asked to attend. The Icelandic authorities, after intervention by the British Embassy, had allowed Anna to be moved to the UK with the proviso that she be sent to a medical institution for rehabilitation.

When her case had come to the courts in Iceland, there had been a great deal of sympathy for her due to the extenuating circumstances and a belief that she had acted in fear of her life, in part due to diminished responsibility. She still firmly believed that she had attacked the car, to stop him following.

We had been allowed to bring her back to the UK, and she had spent the last year in B Wing of the selected prison where she had become an exemplary prisoner. The psychiatrists and medical team were happy with her progress, and there was no belief that she was in any way a danger to the public. It had been circumstance that had forced her into such drastic actions. We would visit her every month, and over time began to see the old Anna emerge from the shell of the person that had come back from Iceland and taken to her new home. At least she recognised us. Michael had never been the same since he first saw her in the hospital, under guard, in Reykjavik. Always a quiet man, he had retreated into himself. Paul did what he could, but it was a lot to ask of a young man. My family and I tried very hard to put it all behind us. Mum and Dad supported everyone best they could.

I also had counselling to help me come to terms with my feelings of guilt for leaving her on the coach and subsequently everything that had happened afterwards. I was assured over and over that, as adults, we all made our own decisions, and who was to know what would happen.

The parole board voted in her favour and she was to be allowed home on licence. She was to have a live-in carer – a nurse – experienced in such circumstances. Michael agreed to all terms. I don't think that their relationship was ever the same again. Even though he knew that everything was against her will, he could not get close to her in any way. They spent much of their time in separate parts of the house. My heart ached for both of them; they had been a very close couple before this tragedy.

I would go to see her most days, and our relationship began to build up again. We never spoke of our time in Iceland, which was a great pity as, up until the kidnapping, we had had a really good time. The photographs we had taken were locked away, but I did occasionally look at them with Adam.

On one of my visits to the house, the TV was on and an advertisement for 4x4 vehicles was on screen. I sprang up to switch it off, but she held my arm, asking me to leave it be. The nurse was in the kitchen, so not present. The car on screen was a black Land Rover-type 4x4. I watched for her reaction.

To my surprise, there was no look of horror, but instead a calmness came over her, and with it, a hint of a smile. It was then that I realised that she knew more than she had ever said. So it was with deep sadness, on my part, that I knew that she knew – and had always known – what she had done.

But we were sisters, and our visits carried on as normal. We never again spoke of the events of that time, not to each other or, in fact, to anyone else. In any case, who was I to allot any blame; her ordeal must have been beyond anything I could imagine. Who knows how anyone would react under such circumstances. His actions were outside of anything that could be expected or tolerated.

You can never really know anyone or anything for certain, but what was certain was he would never do it again.

Acknowledgements

My thanks to Simon Hadfield and Penny Knight for their support in everything.

To Lez Harvey for the cover design.

To Chris Hadfield and Steph Summers for discussions and redesigning any images.

To Christine Emery for being part of my story and for critiques and discussions.

To Gill and Peter Langley for all photographs and information taken from their many travels to Iceland.

To Karen Crick for listening patiently as I mapped out each idea.

To Carl Williams for his technical knowhow.

To friends and work colleagues who listened patiently whilst I regaled them with each stage of the story.

To the hotel staff and various trip guides in Iceland.

To Dean, Tanis, Becky, Julie and all staff at Grosvenor House Publishing Ltd. for their support, advice and encouragement.

To my three cats, Ellie-May, Mali-Blue, and Devon Lacey, listening once again to my ramblings.

Research

Wikipedia, and many travel sites on Iceland.

Map of Icelandic areas.

The Ásbyrgi Visitor Centre

Information on the Icelandic police force, and ICE-SAR Emergency and Rescue Team.

Newspaper reports on an Icelandic kidnapping case.

Other information from own visits to Gullfoss, Old Stokkur, Blue Lagoon, transcontinental plates area, whale watching.

Coach Trips, stormy nights, blizzards, closed-off roads and the cafe up in the hills.

Government sites

British prison system

Women's prisons

British Embassy, Iceland

Icelandic court system

Icelandic prisons

Author information

Nina Olsson lives happily on the Wirral Peninsula with her three cats, her children having left to lead their own interesting lives.

A lover of travel and adventure, the arts, and live music, always involved in some project or other, and ever-ready for the next one.